USBORNE FIRST READING
Level Three

USBORNE FIRST READING

The **Dinosaur** Who Lost His **ROAR**

Russell Punter
Illustrated by Andy Elkerton

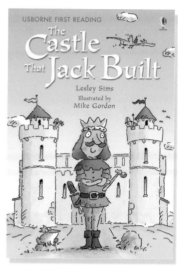

USBORNE FIRST READING

The **Castle** That **Jack Built**

Lesley Sims
Illustrated by Mike Gordon

USBORNE FIRST READING

Chicken Licken

retold by Russell Punter
Illustrated by Ann Kronheimer

USBORNE FIRST READING

The **Three Little Pigs**

retold by Susanna Davidson
Illustrated by Georgien Overwater

2012/12/21

To cutest Talia:

I hope you like this book.

Love,
Mickey

The Leopard
and the
Sky God

Retold by Mairi Mackinnon

Illustrated by
Ali Lodge

Reading Consultant: Alison Kelly
Roehampton University

This story is about

the Sky God,

the
leopard,

his drum,

the python,

the elephant

and the
tortoise.

Long ago, when the world was new,

the animals
lived in the forest.

4

High up above lived
the Sky God.

One day, the Sky God
heard a wonderful sound.

He leaned down and
looked through the trees.

There was the leopard,
playing a great big drum.

He played high

and low.

He played *soft*

and **loud!**

"Hello, Leopard," said the
Sky God.

"Sorry," said the leopard.
He shook his head.

"I'll be very careful," said the Sky God.

"No," said the leopard.

The Sky God waited.

I'll borrow it when he goes hunting.

14

But the leopard kept his
eye on the drum the
whole time.

The Sky God walked away.
"What's the matter?"
asked the other animals.

Leopard won't let me play his drum.

"I wish I had that drum,"
the Sky God said.

"I'll talk to Leopard,"
said the python.

He found the leopard,
playing his drum as usual.

"What do you want?"
growled the leopard.

"May I look at your drum?" asked the python.

The python slithered
away quickly.

"Well?" said the Sky God.
"Sorry," said the python.

"I'm not scared," said the
elephant. "I'll talk to him."

23

He soon heard the drum.
Where was the leopard?

The elephant looked
around. There he was –
up in a tree.

25

"May I look at
your drum?" asked
the elephant.

"Leave me alone!"
roared the leopard.

27

The elephant shook and
shook the tree...

...but he couldn't shake
the leopard out.

"Well?" said the Sky God.
"Sorry," said the elephant.

"Let me try,"
said the tortoise.

29

Now in those days the tortoise had no shell, only a little soft body.

The others laughed.
"You'll never do it."

But the tortoise said,
"Wait and see."

She found the leopard
in his tree.

Mr. Leopard!
Mr. Leopard!

"The Sky God doesn't have a drum," said the leopard.

"It's enormous," said
the tortoise. "He can
climb inside it."

The leopard climbed
down from the tree.

He rolled the drum
along the ground and
crawled inside.

Like this?

"Right inside,"
said the tortoise.

Then she looked around
and spotted the leopard's
cooking pot.

Quickly, she clapped
the lid over the end of
the drum.

40

Then she rolled it along
to the Sky God.

I feel sick!

The Sky God
was very pleased.

I don't want it any more. You can have it.

Thank you!

Then the tortoise said,
"Sky God, can you do
something for me?"

She looked at the drum.
"I would like a shell on
my body...

...so that nothing can hurt me."

"Yes, of course," said the Sky God.

The Sky God loved his drum.

And, when the weather is stormy, you can still hear him...

playing high

and low,

playing *soft*

and **loud!**

The Leopard and the Sky God is a very old story from the Asante kingdom in West Africa (now in the country of Ghana).

Series editor
Lesley Sims

Designed by
Catherine-Anne MacKinnon

First published in 2007 by Usborne Publishing Ltd., Usborne House, 83-85 Saffron Hill, London EC1N 8RT, England. www.usborne.com
Copyright © 2007 Usborne Publishing Ltd.

48

USBORNE FIRST READING
Level Four

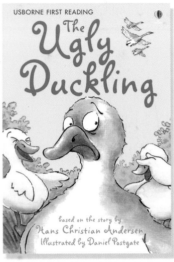

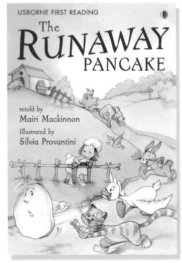